A HIGHWAYMAN FOR CHRISTMAS

CHRISTMAS SCANDALS
BOOK TWO

SUZANNA MEDEIROS

A HIGHWAYMAN FOR CHRISTMAS

Lily Rowland has no choice but to reject the Earl of Seaford's marriage proposal. No one can deny the man is handsome, with his dark hair and dark eyes that flash with a hint of something that lies deeper beneath the surface. But despite the fact they have become good friends, the oh-so-proper earl can never give her what she wants…passion.

Simon took one look at Lily Rowland and knew she'd be his. But after months of resisting the temptation to throw her over his shoulder and carry her to a dark corner to do deliciously wicked things with her, he realizes he's made a tactical error. Because Lily doesn't want the respectable gentleman he's pretending to be. She wants the rake he's hiding from her.

Which leaves him with no choice this Christmas but to kidnap Lily to prove he can give her exactly what she craves.

❄

To learn about Suzanna Medeiros's future books, you can sign up for her newsletter at https://www. suzannamedeiros.com/newsletter.

December 1817

"I'm afraid I cannot accept your proposal."

With those words, an almost deafening silence settled over the room. Lily Rowland had to look away from the man who was seated at the other end of the settee, a respectable amount of space between them. A pang of remorse struck her, and she wanted to snatch back her refusal. Give him another answer.

She liked the Earl of Seaford a great deal. And heaven knew the man was handsome with his dark hair and dark eyes. At times she'd wanted to believe she could feel those fathomless eyes pierce through to her very soul. But those moments were fleeting, a product of her overactive imagination. Lord Seaford had always been circumspect in his behavior toward her, and he'd never once strayed beyond the bounds of social convention.

When he'd taken up residence on a neighboring estate six months ago, the entire area had exploded with speculation. No one knew why the handsome —and wealthy—young earl had chosen to move into one of his smaller holdings in Berkshire. His sister and mother stayed there during the winter months, but he'd never visited.

The resulting gossip when he began to court Lily had run through the neighborhood.

She'd had a disappointing first season that year. Seaford hadn't attended any of the usual events that spring. But they'd met at the very end of the season when Lily and her sisters visited Clara Howe, the earl's sister, before leaving London.

Lily had known his family for several years now since Clara was very close to Lily's youngest sister, Violet. That rainy afternoon in June was the first time she'd met Clara's brother.

When the earl joined his mother and sister in Berkshire, Lily's sisters had teased her relentlessly, saying that Seaford had followed her to the country. And when he'd called on her soon after, Lily realized her sisters were correct. She'd started spinning fantasies about how the handsome and enigmatic Earl of Seaford had taken one look at her on that rainy afternoon in London and decided he wanted her to be his countess.

But Lily's unease only increased with each passing month when it became clear that something vital was missing from the handsome earl's courtship.

He was attentive and everything a young woman could want in a suitor. Everyone would think her mad for turning down his marriage proposal. Without a doubt, her father and her sisters would question her sanity.

But when she thought about her future, Lily wanted what her cousin had found. Beyond the respect and regard of her husband—which Seaford could certainly give Lily—Celia Rowland had Viscount Thornton's love.

Celia had narrowly avoided being caught in a compromising position with Viscount Thornton last Christmas during the dowager viscountess's annual Christmas house party. They'd managed to distract everyone from the speculation about what might have happened when the viscount declared their intention to wed.

Celia had later confessed to Lily that he'd been forced into making that announcement, but it was clear to everyone who saw the two of them together that their relationship had grown beyond that scandal. They were in love. Seeing the way Lord Thornton looked at his wife… Lily wanted that for herself.

She'd hoped to find that with Lord Seaford, but it was clear there would never be heat in his eyes when he looked at her.

She glanced at him again and almost changed her mind when she saw the way his brow furrowed in confusion. Forcing back the urge to reach for his hand and tell him she'd made a horrible mistake, she looked away and took a deep breath.

She'd come to consider the Earl of Seaford a friend. Clara Howe's kind older brother. Friendship in marriage could only be a benefit, but she wanted so much more than that.

Of late, it had become increasingly obvious that something was amiss between them. Maybe turning down his proposal would fix the uncomfortable silences that had become more frequent whenever they were together.

"May I ask why?"

The words were spoken without a hint of emotion, which only served to confirm she'd made the right decision.

"I'd like to think we have become friends over the past few months."

He frowned. "Which means we will suit well in marriage."

She drew in a deep breath, trying to gather courage for what she needed to say. How truthful should she be? For a moment, his eyes dipped to her chest. But when he met her gaze again, there was no evidence of the heat she'd often seen on Lord Thornton's face when he looked at his wife.

She forced the words past her dry throat. "There is more than friendship between a man and a woman in marriage."

He looked away for several seconds. She waited, hoping he would say something—anything—to change her mind. To show her there was more than comfortable companionship between them.

"I can be patient. I'm sure we will… suit… in that area as well."

Disappointment threatened to crush her. She rose to her feet, and he did so as well. Of course he did. Seaford would never flout social conventions.

"We can discuss this again after we're married—"

"No," she said, cutting him off.

His mouth flattened into a line as he waited for her to continue. She wanted him to argue with her, convince her she was wrong about him. But his every action only served to underscore the truth. This man might come to love her, but she feared the emotion would be no different than what he felt for his sister.

"I want passion."

His posture stiffened, but she couldn't regret her outburst. Seaford couldn't give her what she needed, so it was best to let him know in no uncertain terms that her decision was final.

"What do you know of passion?"

His words were clipped, and finally there was a hint of heat in his eyes. If only that heat were directed at her. Instead, she couldn't help but think he was judging her. Perhaps he thought her wanton.

"Personally? Nothing. But that doesn't mean I don't want it. Crave it with every fiber of my being. I want what my cousin Celia has with her husband. I want people to take one look at me and my future husband and know that we are in love."

"I—" He opened his mouth to reply.

She spoke over him. "I know you don't think of me in that way, which is why I must turn down your offer of marriage."

Well, at least she'd finally forced him to drop his polite mask. But what replaced it was cold and more than a little frightening. If she didn't know better, she'd say he was angry with her.

She closed her eyes and took another steadying breath. He hated her now. Perhaps that was for the best. Seaford could never give her what she wanted, and it was time she gave up the fantasies she'd been spinning in her mind about this man.

She expected him to take his leave. Instead, a muscle jumped along his jaw, and he took several steps toward her. Shock held her frozen in place.

She stared up at him, and it was clear now that he was angry. No, furious. But this was Seaford, and he wouldn't hurt her. She stiffened her spine, waiting for him to tell her he'd misjudged her. That she wasn't the type of woman he wanted for a wife.

"I'm going to change your mind."

She stared at him in shock. There were emotions swirling in his eyes now, but she couldn't name them.

Before she could say anything else, he offered her a curt nod and left the room.

She stared after him, an uncomfortable realization settling over her. She had underestimated this man.

She couldn't help but remember her cousin's words when Lily had spoken to her recently. Celia had told her that her husband was concerned about Seaford courting Lily because the man had a reputation for being a rake. She'd dismissed Celia's warning because it didn't seem possible. The Seaford she knew could never be called a rake. But maybe she was wrong?

She dropped onto the settee, dread settling in the pit of her stomach. Her thoughts were mired in confusion. Was it possible she'd only seen one side of the man and that he possessed depths he'd been hiding from her?

No, she thought with a shake of her head. If he was hiding that side of himself, then she should be congratulating herself for having escaped unscathed. Surely only misery would come from being married to a man who thought nothing of throwing himself at all manner of women.

Then why did she want to chase after him?

She jumped when the front door closed with an unnaturally loud bang.

The silence that followed was broken by the

sound of quick footsteps before her sisters burst into the room.

Iris lowered herself onto the settee next to her. "What happened? Did he propose? Father said he was going to ask you today."

Violet sat on Lily's other side. "Did he change his mind? He'd still be here if he asked you… wouldn't he?"

Lily was unable to hold back her tears.

CHAPTER 2

Never had Simon failed in such a spectacular fashion. He'd miscalculated—badly. But he wasn't going to quit the field.

He wanted Lily Rowland, and by God, he would have her.

If Miss Rowland thought him lacking in passion, she would soon learn the opposite was true. Gone was his farce of acting the part of a proper gentleman for her. Gone was his belief that he had to hide who he really was. To hide the fact that he wanted her with a desperation that wasn't gentlemanly. That wasn't nice.

No, from this point forward, he was going to take what he wanted. Lily couldn't know what she was asking for, but he was going to show her that he was more than capable of being passionate. He only hoped she was prepared to discover his true nature.

He stormed into the house, his temper still hot. But he wasn't angry with Lily. No, he was furious with himself. He'd been the worst sort of fool. Somehow he'd convinced himself that he needed to become someone he wasn't in order to gain the hand of the woman he wanted. Instead, he'd driven her away.

He swung the greatcoat from his shoulders and handed it, along with his hat and gloves, to the waiting footman.

"Please ask Hastings to see me in the study."

His words were clipped, and the young man turned immediately to find Simon's valet. At least he hadn't yelled.

He made his way to the study and poured a measure of brandy. It was only afternoon, but given the horrible mess he'd managed to make of his only attempt to woo a woman, no one would blame him for doing what he could to steady his emotions.

The past six months had been a special kind of hell for him. Being so close to the woman he wanted to make his own and forcing himself not to touch her.

At least he hadn't told anyone he planned to propose today. Hastings knew, of course, but his mother and sister expected him to propose at Christmas. That had been his original plan, but he'd become impatient. He wanted the matter of courting Lily behind him so he could have her as his wife. In his home and, more importantly, in his bed.

He'd given up all female companionship after meeting Lily earlier this year. He didn't regret that decision. He'd had his fill of women for years now, but Lily was the only gently bred young woman he'd met who stirred the beast within.

At first, he thought it was her beauty that captivated him, which had seemed odd. He'd met all manner of eligible young women who were as beautiful, perhaps even more so than her. But his instincts all sprang to attention when Clara introduced him to her good friend's oldest sister.

Those instincts had told him that the young woman standing before him, her blond hair curling about her face, her blue eyes gleaming with appreciation—nothing he hadn't seen before in countless other women—would belong to him. And not just for one night but forever.

He tossed back his drink and began to pace.

That was how his valet found him several minutes later.

Hastings rapped softly at the door and then let himself in without waiting for an invitation. He took one look at Simon and sighed.

"I take it this afternoon did not go as you'd hoped."

Simon laughed; he couldn't help it. The situation was absurd. "I am a case study in irony."

Hastings's brows rose. "That means…?"

"She refused me because she thinks we're *friends* and she wants *passion*." The words sounded bitter on his tongue. "Apparently she doesn't think she can get that with me."

He gave his valet credit for not laughing at him.

"You're not a man to give up so easily."

"Of course not. I'm going to give her exactly what she wants." One corner of his mouth lifted as he thought about all the ways he could show Lily that he was more than up to the challenge she'd laid before him. "She's thrown down the gauntlet, and I am honor bound to show her that I am more than capable of giving her exactly what she wants."

"Of course you are, my lord."

Simon ignored the hint of dryness in his valet's tone. The man had been with him for enough years to know that the one area in which the Earl of Seaford was *not* lacking was in passion.

His smile turned into a full grin as a plan began to form in his mind. "I'm going to need your help."

Hastings inclined his head. "Just say the word."

CHAPTER 3

ily slipped into the morning room to find that her sisters were already hiding there.

Father had been in a grumpy mood all day. It was now midafternoon, and soon they'd be leaving.

Normally the three of them spent their time in that room gossiping about what was happening in the neighborhood while working on their needlework and drawing. But a dark cloud had settled over the house on what should have been a happy day.

Violet and Iris were standing side by side next to the window and turned at her entrance.

Iris let out a sigh. "It doesn't appear that it will snow."

"No." Violet's shoulders slumped. "We'll be

trapped in the carriage, listening to Father's complaints the whole way to Lord Seaford's estate."

Lily winced, guilt stabbing at her. "Father never liked house parties. I don't know why he agreed to attend this one."

Iris tilted her head to one side. "Do you not? We all thought you were going to marry the earl. So of course when his mother and sister invited us to spend a few days with them before Christmas, he jumped at the opportunity."

"He didn't precisely jump," Lily said, remembering the reluctance with which their father had agreed to go with them.

"Given his reaction last year when we suggested he join us for the Dowager Viscountess Thornton's annual Christmas gathering, it was as good as an exclamation of joy."

Lily sat in one of the hard, high-back chairs that were placed around the table they used for their various projects. "I feel terrible about this. I hope you'll manage to have fun anyway. Clara will be there, and I know how well the three of you get along."

Violet dropped into the chair next to her. "Please tell us you've changed your mind."

Violet bit her lip as she waited for Lily's reply,

and another stab of guilt went through Lily. "That is not how proposals of marriage are done. Lord Seaford asked, and I answered. I can't just invite myself to the man's home and then tell him I've changed my mind."

And especially not when she feared he would laugh in her face. But that didn't matter because, as she'd told herself countless times whenever she thought of that day one week ago, she'd made the right decision.

Violet let out a loud sigh. "I was so looking forward to this visit. Spending a few days with Clara would have been wonderful before…"

Violet didn't need to finish her sentence. *Before you ruined everything*.

"Clara is still your friend. Nothing will change that."

But now Father was going to a house party at the Seaford estate, something which he detested. And to make the entire situation worse, his sacrifice would be for naught because his daughter wasn't going to be the next countess.

When Lily refused the earl's proposal, they'd all expected that a polite excuse would be made for canceling the gathering. The Rowlands were the only guests, after all.

Instead, they'd received a short note to say that the earl was sending his carriage to collect them. After dropping off Iris, Violet, and their father at the Seaford estate, it would take Lily, alone, to the Thornton's annual Christmas house party.

Apparently Seaford hated her so much he'd gone out of his way to make it clear she was no longer welcome in his home. Her heart clenched whenever she thought about the curt note written in his slashing handwriting in black ink.

The door swung open, and they all turned to find their father standing on the threshold, his forehead furrowed in a frown.

"Are the three of you planning to stay in here forever? The carriage has arrived." He turned and strode from the room.

It would take some time for Father to forgive her. At least Iris and Violet weren't angry with her, but their misery was clear.

SEAFORD'S CARRIAGE WAS FAR MORE LUXURIOUS than their own serviceable conveyance. A small brazier was already lit, supplying just enough warmth to hold the cold weather at bay. Lily had never ridden in such comfort.

In contrast, the atmosphere within the vehicle was tense. Lily spent most of the trip looking out one of the windows while her sisters did the same. Father, however, sat there with a frown etched onto his face.

He didn't speak until they turned onto the private drive that led to the Seaford estate. "You should have told me you weren't going to accept him. It would have saved me the embarrassment of agreeing to this event."

Iris and Violet both inhaled sharply, but Father continued, turning to them. "The two of you still could have visited with Miss Howe. But there's no reason for me to be here. It's going to be damn awkward."

Lily winced as he said the last words. His harsh language was a testament to just how upset he was. Father never swore in their presence.

She looked away, unable to think of anything she could say to explain her reasoning. She'd had reservations about Seaford's courtship for some time and had even spoken to her cousin Celia about them. She could hardly tell her father that she couldn't accept Seaford's proposal because their courtship had been far too proper. She couldn't admit that she wanted to be swept off her feet. Potentially even have the man try to seduce her. At the very least, he should have tried to kiss her after six months of courtship.

She tried not to think about Celia's warning that Seaford had a reputation for being a rake. That only made his propriety worse. She couldn't help but believe he'd settled on her as a suitable candidate to be his wife but that he didn't actually *want* her.

The carriage drew to a halt, and a footman opened the door. Although she wasn't staying, Lily exited the vehicle as well. Ignoring the heavy weight that had settled in the pit of her stomach, she turned to greet the family.

Clara was Seaford's only sibling, and she rushed forward to hug Violet, then Iris, and finally Lily. The dowager countess smiled fondly at her daughter's happiness before greeting them all.

"My son sends his apologies," she said, her mouth turning down slightly. "He's had to return to London and isn't currently in residence."

She then turned to Lily and clasped one of her hands between hers. "I was sorry to hear you'd already promised your cousin you'd be joining them again this year. We were looking forward to having you here. It would have given me time to get to know you better and no doubt would have served as an inducement for my son to remain in Berkshire."

Lily was speechless for several seconds before finally murmuring something about being disappointed she couldn't join them this year.

It was clear Lady Seaford didn't know what had happened between Lily and her son. She didn't know that Seaford had already proposed and been refused.

For one moment, her heart soared as she thought that perhaps he hadn't given up on her. But then Lily chided herself for continuing to spin fantasy scenarios that were never going to take place.

If Seaford wanted another chance to woo her, he wouldn't have returned to London. And the fact that he'd personally made arrangements for her to spend this period before Christmas at the Thornton estate meant he didn't want her under his roof at all. That was the action of a man who wanted no connection between her and his family.

She stood off to the side as the trunks were unloaded. Then, after only a few minutes, it was time to say her goodbyes to everyone.

Lady Seaford turned to her. "We're sending along another servant who will ride outside with the driver. The roads between here and the Thornton estate are safe, and the journey isn't a long one, but we wanted to put your mind at ease. It's never easy to travel alone."

Lily hugged her sisters and Clara, then dipped into a curtsy before Lady Seaford.

When she turned to her father, she didn't expect to see the compassion on his face. He understood the import of the earl's actions—Lily was banished from the house. Over the years, she'd spent much time here, but those days were now at an end. Soon Lady Seaford would learn that Lily would never be her daughter-in-law.

Tears pricked at her eyes as a footman helped her into the carriage, but Lily refused to let them fall. She'd made her decision and now must live with the consequences.

She took a deep breath before pasting on a smile and turning to wave goodbye through the window.

Everything would work out in the end. Her disappointment was temporary and soon she'd be able to put it behind her. At least she could console herself with the fact that her actions hadn't cost Iris and Violet their friendship with Clara. And one day, when Seaford wed, he would no longer care about her at all and she'd be able to visit as well.

A sharp stab of pain threatened to steal her breath at the thought of Seaford marrying another woman. With great difficulty, she leaned back against the plush cushions and tried to think of something—anything—other than Seaford's future countess.

They traveled for some time before Lily opened her eyes again and gazed outside at the passing scenery. She'd hoped to find solace in sleep, but her morose thoughts refused to leave her.

She frowned when she didn't recognize the road. Where were they? It stood to reason that she wouldn't recognize this road. She'd never made the trip to the Thornton estate from anywhere other than her own home. Still, they should be approaching the manse soon. The estate wasn't that far from Seaford's.

She was about to tap on the roof to ask how much longer it would be until they reached their destination but hesitated. Instead, she cried out when they jolted to a halt. Another glance outside the window told her that they definitely hadn't reached the Thornton estate.

"Why have we stopped?" she called out, worried they might have gone over a rut in the road that damaged the carriage.

The door was flung open, and a dark figured blocked out the light. The sun was behind the man, so she couldn't tell if this was the driver or the man accompanying them to ensure her safety.

She realized it was neither when the man pulled out a pistol and aimed it at her.

CHAPTER 4

$\mathcal{A}$nticipation surged through Simon's veins. The plans he'd carefully set in motion were now underway. There was no doubt in his mind that he shouldn't be so excited about his course of action, but it was time he started behaving true to form again.

Lily said she wanted passion, and he was going to show her she could have that with him. Acting the part of a gentleman hadn't won her hand, so now he would show her who he was. She needed to see that he'd been playing a role for the past six months.

He wasn't meek when it came to women. He let them know exactly what he wanted from them, and for the most part, they were more than willing to go along with whatever he suggested.

But Lily was a maiden and younger than him by eight years. Granted, he wouldn't be thirty for three more years, so he wasn't exactly old, but he had never been with someone younger than twenty. Normally his dalliances were with women his age or a little older. It was surprising how many widows were not yet thirty, but given the penchant of older men to wed women who were barely out of the schoolroom, he supposed it was to be expected. He'd had a mistress a few years ago but got tired of even that level of commitment.

Which was why he'd been shaken to realize that he didn't just want Lily in his bed, but he wanted to keep her at his side. Ensure that she was his alone.

When he'd inherited his title a few years ago, after his father had suffered an apoplexy, he'd known he couldn't put off marriage forever. But he hadn't felt the need to find a bride just yet. Whenever he did think about marrying, he'd assumed it would be to someone older, more experienced in the ways of lovemaking. Someone who could hold his interest long term.

Lily had taken him by surprise, and he couldn't say why she'd captured his interest so thoroughly.

Perhaps some part of him had recognized the hidden depths of her personality, the side of her that craved passion. But because she was an innocent, he'd hidden that side of himself from her. Acted the part of what he thought a true gentleman should be.

He would have saved so much time if he'd been himself.

He'd have to find some way to reward his valet, who'd made most of the arrangements for today. Hastings had mapped out exactly how long it would take the Rowlands to reach his estate. Seaford had also asked Hastings to escort the carriage after it left his estate. Hastings had served in the British army when he was younger and could handle himself in any situation. Lily would be safe with his valet escorting her.

Hastings had also undertaken the task of convincing the carriage driver to go along with their plan. That had involved Seaford speaking to the man and explaining exactly what he planned to do. The driver had been understandably nervous about getting involved with the scheme.

Simon had given him his word that no harm would come to Miss Rowland. He didn't know exactly what Hastings had told the man, but he had the impression it was something about Miss Rowland thinking that her suitor was boring and that the earl needed to show her he was anything but boring. Neither man said as much to him, but the driver had made a comment about women who read too much wanting romantic adventures.

He pulled out his pocket watch for what seemed to be the hundredth time as he remained hidden in a small wooded area. Right on schedule, his carriage turned onto the small road that ran alongside his hiding spot.

His body surged with excitement. He'd arrived early, of course, not wanting to take any chance he'd miss the carriage. It wasn't snowing, but it was deuced cold.

He pulled his domino into place—thank heaven for masked balls—and raised the hood of his coat over his head. He didn't know where Hastings had found the garment, but it was large enough to envelop his frame. It wouldn't be obvious that it was him, especially with the hood up and his mask in place.

He had a moment of concern as the carriage came to a sudden halt. He only hoped his assessment of this young woman was correct and that she wouldn't faint or do anything that would make him feel like a monster. The last thing he wanted to do was frighten Lily.

He crossed the space to the carriage, not looking at the two men.

"Why have we stopped?" Lily called out from inside the vehicle. He took a deep breath, his pulse hammering in his ears, and flung open the carriage door. Then he pulled out the unloaded pistol he was carrying and pointed it at her.

"Get out of the carriage."

LILY'S HEART THUNDERED, AND FOR A MOMENT SHE feared she was going to faint. She took a deep breath as she tried to hold back her panic. It would do no good to succumb to hysterics.

She found it odd when the highwayman bent to pull down the carriage steps. Why would a man who'd taken up such a dishonorable profession politely step back and wait for her to exit?

She expected to see the driver and his companion standing near the front of the carriage. Her gaze careened about wildly, and then she looked up. The two men were still seated on the bench.

Surely a thief would have secured his two greatest threats before asking her to exit.

And then the unthinkable happened. The carriage began to move.

"Wait—" she called out, unwilling to believe what was happening. They were saving themselves by leaving her behind.

Thinking only that she needed to get back into that carriage, she lifted her skirts and started to run after it. She made it only two steps before the high-wayman pulled her back against him. Shock raced through her as she struggled in his grasp.

"You have my word that I'm not going to hurt you." His voice was low and far too close.

She could only stare after the carriage as it disappeared from view, her stomach hollowing out with fear. "The reassurance of a brigand holds no meaning."

CHAPTER 5

e barely held back a laugh. It shouldn't have surprised him that this woman's sharp wit would assert itself now. Still, he wanted to ease her distress, so he stuffed the pistol into a coat pocket.

He loosened his hold and turned her to face him. He kept his hands on her upper arms, though. The last thing he wanted was for Lily to hurt herself while trying to flee.

She took a deep breath and then lifted her face, taking a good look at him for the first time. Her eyes roamed over his face. His hair was covered with the black hood, but the domino he wore only concealed the upper part of his face. Surely she would recognize him before he had to reveal his identity.

After several seconds, her eyes narrowed, a slight crease forming between her brows. He wanted to drop a kiss on that line.

"Do we… know one another?"

"Why don't you find out?"

He released one of her arms and waited to see what she would do. She took another deep, shuddering breath before reaching for his face with a hand that was, thankfully, steady. How he wanted her to caress him with that hand, but that would have to wait for another time.

Lily pushed back the hood and then raised the domino to his forehead. Her eyes widened, and she sucked in a breath.

"Seaford?"

He couldn't hold back his grin. "Were you expecting someone else?"

"What…? How…?" She stamped a foot and tugged on the arm he still held. He released her, hoping she would no longer feel the need to run away from him.

"What is the meaning of this? Your mother said you were in London."

"You wanted passion, Lily." It was the first time he'd called her by her given name, and her small inhalation told him she'd taken note of that fact.

"I'm going to show you that I can give you everything you want and more."

Enjoying the way her mouth dropped open, he bent and swept her into his arms. She flung her hands around his neck but said nothing.

He kept his eyes on the path ahead, refusing to be distracted by her weight in his arms and the feel of her soft curves pressing against him.

When he reached the group of trees behind which he'd left his horse, he lowered her to her feet again. He untied the black gelding and mounted into the saddle. Realizing that the mask he'd donned was still pushed up on his forehead, he took a moment to remove it and stuffed it into a pocket. Then he leaned down and held his hand out to her.

She shook her head, her breath coming out in little puffs in the cold air. "You can't expect me to get on that horse with you."

It took a little effort to school his expression so she wouldn't see his amusement. "I'd make a poor highwayman if I went to all this trouble to gain my prize and then left her alone in the country, far away from anyone who could assist her."

Her brows drew together in a frown. She wanted to refuse him, so he continued. "It will be evening soon. And if you haven't noticed, it's starting to get colder. I think it might snow."

She let out a huff of exasperation and then placed her hand in his. "How are we going to manage this?"

Grinning, he leaned down to capture her under her arms. Ignoring the fact that his thumbs were very close to her breasts, he lifted her with ease. Again, she grasped him around his neck as he arranged her sideways on the horse in front of him. It wouldn't be comfortable for her, but they didn't have a long ride ahead.

When she didn't release her tight grasp on his neck, he leaned back slightly to look down at her. Lily's eyes were scrunched closed, her mouth pressed in a tight line. It took every ounce of strength he possessed not to try to distract her with a kiss. When he finally kissed this woman, she would want it as much as he did.

He took hold of her arms, and she allowed him to unwrap them from his neck and place them around his waist.

"Don't drop me," she said as she pressed herself closer.

"Never."

CHAPTER 6

*L*ily wouldn't swoon, but heavens, how she wanted to. She almost expected to open her eyes and discover she was dreaming.

The Earl of Seaford had kidnapped her!

Her emotions were a tangled mess as she tried to come to terms with the day's unexpected turn. She'd feared this man hated her and didn't want her anywhere near him or his family, but clearly that wasn't true.

I'm going to change your mind.

He'd said those words to her after she refused his proposal. She'd be lying if she said she hadn't hoped for something—anything—to show her that he cared for her. That he could give her the passion she craved. But a large part of her found it impossible to believe the circumspect gentleman who'd been courting her for months now would behave in such a way.

She let out a soft breath. No, he had to be playing a role, hoping to change her mind by quite literally sweeping her off her feet. And if he succeeded, it was likely he'd revert to his normal staid self.

But that didn't mean she shouldn't enjoy this little adventure while she had the opportunity.

If she was thinking logically instead of giving her romantic yearnings free rein, she would be afraid right now. But despite how much she tried to convince herself she needed to proceed with caution, she didn't believe this man would harm her.

She settled against him, enjoying the way his muscled chest felt beneath her cheek. Their position was born of practical necessity, but it was impossible not to revel in the fact that this man who had kept her at arm's length for so long was finally allowing her to get close.

She couldn't hold back her thrill of anticipation as she considered what might happen over the next few days. But if this man thought he only had to kidnap her and she would swoon at his feet, he was mistaken. If Seaford wanted her, he was going to have to win her.

Butterflies rioted in her belly at being held so intimately in Seaford's arms. Somehow, she resisted the urge to run her hands up his back. He was stronger than she'd imagined, given the way he'd easily lifted her onto the horse. She didn't think he would drop her, but she wouldn't risk distracting him.

She stayed still, enjoying the heat that emanated from his body. He'd drawn the edges of his coat over her smaller frame, and between that extra layer of wool and the man himself, she wasn't cold.

The ride wasn't long, perhaps five minutes in total, when he brought the horse to a stop. She didn't move right away, her thoughts racing as she wondered what was going to happen now.

"We've arrived, Lily." His voice was low, spoken near her ear.

He brought one hand up to her back and ran it up and down her spine. Shivers raced through her at the intimate touch. She leaned back. His brows were wrinkled in concern as he met her gaze.

Well, good. He could have frightened her to death with the events he'd set in motion today. At the very least, she could have fainted from fear.

Not that she'd ever fainted—not even when one of the stable's cats continued to bring her dead mice whenever she went riding. Iris and Violet usually asked the groom to bring their mounts outside after he'd done it the first time, but Lily knew the cat just wanted to show off his hunting prowess.

She licked her lips and noticed the way his eyes zeroed in on her mouth. "Where did you bring me?"

"Somewhere quiet where we can get to know one another."

She frowned. "I already know you, my lord."

He shook his head. "You think you know me. But that man you rejected—and rightfully so— wasn't the real me."

She should be alarmed at that statement. Her cousin's words rang in her ears again—the warning from Celia's husband that Seaford was a rake. Instead, she couldn't deny that his words had the opposite effect.

She didn't say anything as he helped her down from the horse and then swung from the saddle.

He held out his hand, and with a deep inhale, she took it. He smiled down at her before leading her and the horse to a small building that was just big enough to keep his mount safe from the elements.

She stood quietly to one side as he removed the saddle and then set about rubbing the animal down. She had to admit she enjoyed watching Seaford work. He didn't falter, and it was clear he'd done this often. She wondered how many other nobles could care for their own horses. She didn't think it was a skill that many possessed.

Finally he brought the black horse to a stall that had already been stocked with feed. He rubbed the animal's nose and whispered words of praise when the horse leaned into his touch. Lily couldn't stop remembering how good it had felt when he'd rubbed that same hand along her spine only minutes before.

Heat rose in her cheeks, and she turned away, knowing that Seaford's attention would soon be returning to her. If there was a small building for stabling a horse here, there would also be a dwelling. Which meant there would be servants even if there was no groom.

The knowledge that there would be witnesses to her current situation, more than anything else that had happened today, had her cringing with embarrassment.

CHAPTER 7

After seeing to his horse, Simon led the way to the small cottage that was tucked away in a small wooded area near the edge of his Berkshire estate. At one time it was used as a hunting box, but that was before he'd purchased the estate for his mother, who had grown up in the area.

His valet had made the arrangements to have it cleaned and stocked for a short stay. Hastings had used the excuse that Seaford liked to get away for a few days of outdoor exercise and that it should always be kept ready for his use.

Their stay here wouldn't be long. He couldn't keep Lily hidden away in the country indefinitely even though the thought was appealing. When her family returned home a few days from now, they would expect Lily to also be on her way.

He'd almost reached the small stone cottage when he noticed Lily was no longer following him. He turned to find she'd halted several feet away and was gazing at the house with a hint of alarm. Her hands were clasping her upper arms, and she was shivering.

"You should come in; you're cold. There's a fire in the main room, and I can assure you it's much warmer inside than it is out here."

She bit her lower lip, her eyes fixed on the house. "Who else lives here?"

"No one. This cottage is still on my property."

She shook her head. "I mean the servants," she said, keeping her voice low. "Who will know that I'm here, alone with you?"

He crossed the space that separated them and stopped when she was within reach. He wanted to draw her into his arms to stop her shivering but restrained himself. He was getting quite good at keeping his baser instincts at bay.

"No one. It will be just you and me."

She considered his words before nodding. He held out his hand for her, but this time she didn't take it. Instead, she walked past him toward the cottage, her back ramrod straight. She stopped before the worn wooden door and turned to face him again. "What's going to happen once I cross that threshold?"

He met her gaze. "Nothing that you don't want to happen. But…"

She licked her lips, and he wanted to groan. "But?"

He was long past pretending to be circumspect with this woman. "I'm hoping I'll be able to give you *everything*."

She swallowed visibly and stepped aside. He opened the door and again held out his hand. When she placed her hand in his, he tightened his fingers around them and led her into the cottage.

Heat engulfed them as they stepped into the front room. It was a small building that had only two rooms on the main floor—a front room and a kitchen—and two bedrooms on the second floor.

He was glad he'd taken the time to stoke the fire before leaving to meet the carriage. It had dwindled down, so he took off his coat and hung it on one of the hooks that had been placed by the front door for just that purpose. He removed his gloves and strode to the fireplace to add more wood to the fire.

When he was satisfied it would continue to keep

the small cottage warm, he turned to face Lily. He'd been slow and careful with her, knowing that he needed to give her time to get used to the situation in which she now found herself. He wasn't surprised to see she'd found the pistol he'd tucked away into one of the pockets of the voluminous coat and now stood with it pointed at him. Lily was clever, which was one of the things he'd always liked about her. She wasn't going to allow this opportunity to pass.

"You're going to take me to the Thornton estate. They're expecting me and will be worried when I don't arrive."

He took a step toward her. "No one is expecting you, Lily."

It only took her a moment to realize the truth. "Of course not. That was a lie. A way to get me away from my family so they wouldn't worry about me when you…" The pistol began to lower, but then she squared her shoulders and raised it again. "It doesn't matter. You can take me to see my cousin Celia or return me to your estate. Given the circumstances, I don't think you can continue to banish me from your home."

It was time for him to show her his hand. "I want you to be my countess and mistress of all my houses. I apologize for making you believe I didn't want you there, but it was necessary to carry out the task at hand."

Her mouth firmed into a thin line before she spoke. "The task of kidnapping me."

He took another step closer.

"Stay where you are." Her hand shook, and for a moment he wondered if she would pull the trigger.

"We only have one horse, my dear. How can I take you anywhere if I don't come near you?"

Her nose scrunched as she considered his words. Finally she let out a soft huff and lowered the pistol.

He closed the space between them and took the weapon from her hands. Then he pointed it at the ceiling and pulled the trigger.

Nothing happened.

"You… you…," she sputtered as she tried to think of an accusation to level at him.

He raised a hand and ran the back of a finger along her jaw. "It was never loaded, Lily. Did you think I would take a chance with anything that might harm you?"

She was silent for several moments. "Honestly? No. But I also never thought you'd do something like this."

A pang of guilt hit him square in the chest. "You have driven me to take desperate action."

She shook her head. "If anyone learns that the two of us were alone here together, I will be ruined." She frowned. "Is that what you're planning to do? Cause a scandal and force my hand?"

She was gazing up at him, her eyes never leaving his. As though she were trying to read his thoughts.

"I would never force you to do anything you don't want to do, and that includes marrying me." He stepped closer and leaned down so his face was inches from hers. "I give you fair warning that I will try to seduce you. But it is *you* who will have the final say in anything that happens between us."

She swallowed visibly and leaned closer to him. He didn't think she'd done so consciously, and he was tempted to act on the unspoken invitation. But not yet. It was too soon.

He dropped his hand from her cheek and took a step back. Her small pout of disappointment was gratifying.

"If you're hungry, there is food in the kitchen. But I'm afraid my skills there only go as far as setting out a cold meal that someone else has prepared."

Her head tilted to one side. "Please tell me there's tea."

"If not, someone on my staff will receive a stern reprimand."

Her smile lifted his heart, and together they made their way to the kitchen.

CHAPTER 8

*L*ily watched him as he set about unpacking the small picnic basket that had been left for them, spreading the wrapped packages of food on the small square table.

He darted a quick look her way. "Are you going to make the tea?"

"I was waiting to see if you would need help."

He crossed over to a cupboard and looked inside. "I found the plates and cutlery, so I think I'll be able to manage this."

With a small shake of her head, she turned and set the water to heat. As she prepared the kettle, her thoughts went over the events of the day. She no longer believed she was dreaming. Her imagination would never have been able to dream up the current situation in which she found herself.

She'd enjoyed sneaking into the kitchen to watch the staff go about their duties when she was younger and she knew what to do. It didn't hurt that their matronly cook would gift her with biscuits so she visited often.

She couldn't help but wonder if Seaford truly believed they could spend the next few days here alone. He was an earl and had several estates filled with servants who saw to his every need. It wouldn't take long for him to tire of cold meals.

She was so deep into her musings that she didn't notice Seaford had finished and was now watching her. When she turned back to the table after the tea was ready, he was leaning against a wall, his arms folded across his chest. His gaze was lowered—had he been staring at her backside? There was a look on his face that she'd never seen before, one that had her heart beginning to race.

His eyes rose to meet hers. He had the audacity to shrug as though he'd done nothing more than sneak into the kitchens to have a taste of the dessert that was going to be served with dinner.

Deciding that the best course of action was to

ignore the subject altogether, she brought the kettle to the table. He'd done a good job setting out the dinnerware and cutlery. A variety of cold meats, cheeses and bread were unpacked onto serving platters.

He moved behind her and held out her chair, unconcerned that he was taking on the role of a footman. Without a word she sank into it, her legs now a little unsteady, and waited for him to take the chair across the table.

When he was settled, she busied herself with pouring their tea, a sudden shyness settling over her. She already knew he took his without milk or sugar. After she passed him his cup, he waited for her to prepare her plate before doing the same.

"Do you think we'll have snow before Christmas?"

She couldn't help it, she burst out laughing. The entire situation was so ridiculous. This man had kidnapped her, spirited her away to a tiny cottage where it would be just the two of them without even one servant, and now he was talking about the weather?

His laughter joined hers, and she realized he'd been hoping to ease the tension between them with humor. It had worked.

"You didn't bring me here to exchange social niceties with me, my lord."

The corners of his mouth were still turned up in a fond smile, but there was heat in his eyes. Before today she'd caught glimpses of that, look but he'd always been quick to hide it. So quick that she thought she'd been imagining it. But in that moment, he was no longer trying to hide what he was feeling.

"We have time to talk about that later. I don't want to overwhelm you on the first night."

The way his voice dropped on the word *night* caused a shiver to run through her.

They spoke very little throughout the meal. She ignored that logical inner voice that told her she should be pressing him for details about what he was hoping to accomplish with this whole scheme. Because he was right in thinking she wasn't ready to have this conversation with him. Her thoughts and emotions were all in a jumble, and she needed a little bit of time to fully absorb everything that had happened.

When they'd finished eating, they moved in sync and began to pack away the food that remained. She washed their dishes and was shocked when he joined in to help her dry and put them away.

That task done, she turned to face him.

"I'll be back in a moment," he said before snatching up the basket and striding from the room. He opened the cottage's main door and stepped outside.

She clasped her hands at her waist, curious about what he was doing. He returned a minute later with a trunk. Her trunk.

She shook her head. Of course it was. This man had planned everything with care, so it wasn't hard to believe he'd also arranged for her belongings to be brought to the cottage.

She followed him upstairs, bemused by the fact that the so-very-proper earl she'd come to know had morphed into this man who now seemed to be a stranger.

He walked into one of the two bedrooms on the second floor and placed the small trunk on the floor. Lily hadn't packed many belongings since she was only supposed to be gone for three days.

She stayed in the hallway, nervous about being alone with Seaford in a bedroom. This man had never even kissed her, so she imagined she'd be safe with him, but there were some boundaries she wasn't yet ready to cross. Perhaps that would change by the end of their time together.

Heat rose to her cheeks as she thought about all the things that might change before she returned home.

She expected Seaford to say good night and leave her, but instead, he joined her in the hallway. He raised one hand and placed his fingers, still cold from his time outside, on her chin.

"I'm giving you fair warning, Lily. I won't do anything that you don't want me to do, but I do plan to do everything in my power to seduce you."

She didn't know what to say to that and so said nothing as their gazes held for what seemed an eternity. When his eyes lowered to her mouth, she knew what he wanted before he spoke.

"I'm going to kiss you. If you don't want that, tell me."

Now that this moment was here, Lily found that she didn't need to summon the bravery she thought she'd need. She'd wanted Seaford to kiss her so many times over the past few months, and a thrill of anticipation went through her. She'd been longing for more than friendship with this man and had feared it would never come to pass.

She licked her lips and couldn't help but notice the way his eyes narrowed on that small movement. "Yes."

He needed no further prodding. He lowered his head, and finally his mouth settled on hers. Soft and sweet, his lips brushed over hers. She exhaled a soft breath. This was nice.

His hands cupped her cheeks, and she reached at the same time for his upper arms. Not because she wanted to push him away but because she wanted to keep him close.

The press of his mouth became firmer, and then his tongue darted out to trace along the seam of her lips. She opened her mouth for him without prodding, knowing that this was how people kissed and wanting very much to experience it.

With a soft groan, he took the invitation, and his tongue swept into her mouth.

She'd never kissed a man before and thought she wouldn't know what to do. But some instinct had her mirroring his movements, allowing this kiss to go further than she knew he'd intended.

Fire coursed through her body as she realized she would give this man anything he wanted. He need only ask for it.

And then, before she was ready, it was over. He raised his head, and they stared at one another, their breathing labored.

"I'm going to stop now while I still can. We'll

have time enough to get to know one another better tomorrow."

He turned and, without looking back at her, made his way to the stairs.

She watched him as he descended. With a sigh of contentment, she entered the bedroom and closed the door. She leaned against it, her mouth widening in a grin.

She'd been expecting to spend the next few days alone with her cousin and all the guests who would be at the Thornton's house party. She knew Celia would go out of her way to make the visit an enjoyable one, but she'd been dreading it.

But instead of spending the next few days as an outcast from her family and from Seaford's, everything was bright and new.

The future held a world of promise.

CHAPTER 9

When Lily opened her eyes the next morning, it took her a moment to remember where she was. Her bedroom walls weren't yellow, and the morning sun didn't stream through her tall windows at home.

Then yesterday's events came crashing back to her.

Trying not to think about the fact that the carriage driver and the man who'd accompanied him knew she was here, alone with Seaford, she threw back the blankets and rose from the bed. She'd have to trust he'd chosen his accomplices wisely and that no one else would learn he'd kidnapped her.

Because at some point during the night she'd

decided she was going to embrace this adventure with both hands. If Seaford was the proper, emotionless gentleman she'd thought him, he would have moved on and chosen another woman to court. Instead, he'd chosen to show her that he was more than capable of giving her what she craved.

Eager to see what would happen today, Lily moved to where her trunk was lying open at the foot of her bed. She hadn't unpacked it last night when she'd taken out her nightgown, but she did so now. She hung her dresses in the wardrobe that was standing in one corner of the room and placed everything else in the dresser.

With that task behind her, she chose a bright yellow dress to wear today—noting with a smile that it matched the walls of her bedroom. She'd anticipated having to share a maid with several other guests, as she'd done last year when she and her sisters had attended the Thornton house party. With that in mind, she'd selected dresses that didn't button up the back.

Grateful her foresight meant she'd be able to dress herself without the assistance of a maid, she set about preparing for the day ahead.

She sighed as she stood before the mirror. There would be no fancy hairstyle today. She undid the plaits she normally wore when she went to bed and swept her hair up into a serviceable style.

She considered adding one of the hair combs she'd brought with her, but in the end decided against it. The earl had seen her dressed up for his visits. If he was earnest about wanting to marry her, he should know what she looked like when she wasn't going out of her way to impress others. She knew that most women would call her a fool for thinking that, but she saw it as yet another small test of Seaford's character.

Trying to tamp down the excitement that was beginning to grow within her, she made her way downstairs.

Only to find the front room and kitchen empty.

She shook her head and tried to push aside her disappointment. The earl would have to wake up at some point. Until then, she could make herself a pot of tea.

That task complete a few minutes later, she was about to prepare a cup when the unmistakable sound of the front door opening, then closing, almost caused her to drop the teacup.

She turned to the kitchen door, hoping it was Seaford who'd gone outside. But if it wasn't, she couldn't hide. The stairs were in the front room, and there was no other door in the kitchen.

She listened to the sounds of someone moving around in the other room and sent up a silent prayer that it wasn't one of the men who knew about her presence here. She wouldn't be able to face them.

She let out her breath when Seaford stepped into the doorway.

His gaze raked over her form, and she held herself still under his appraisal. This was her, Lily, without the usual finery.

She took the opportunity to appraise him as well. He wore buff-colored trousers and a simple dark blue waistcoat, but he wasn't wearing his customary topcoat. And his jaw had the beginnings of a beard which should have made him appear unkempt but somehow only accentuated the line of his jaw in a most becoming way.

When she met his gaze, he was grinning at her. The moment stretched taut between them before he broke the silence.

"I see you've made tea. Bless you."

He raised his arm to show her the basket that contained the remains of their meal from the night before. He must have kept it outside so the cold air would keep the food from spoiling.

"Did we leave enough to eat today?"

He shook his head. "I'm afraid not, but my valet dropped off another picnic basket for us."

She winced. "How many people know I'm here with you?"

"Just him and the carriage driver," he said, moving farther into the room and beginning to unpack their morning meal. "I was outside caring for my horse when he stopped by. I've been assured there is enough food to last us the rest of the day."

She brought the teapot to the table and then helped him to set out the plates and cutlery. She supposed it made sense that Seaford's personal servant was the man who'd joined them yesterday. If the earl knew the man well, that would explain why he was confident he could be trusted.

Like yesterday, Seaford helped her into the chair, and she poured their tea.

She cut thick slices of still-warm bread for the two of them and slathered a good amount of fresh butter on hers. Normally she liked toast and eggs for breakfast, but she wouldn't complain. Seaford was going to a great deal of trouble to see to their needs while also ensuring their privacy.

She took a bite, watching the way Seaford devoured his own bread and cut himself another slice. "So tell me about this cottage. Have you kidnapped any other women and brought them here?"

His grin held a hint of wickedness as he added jam to his second slice. "Only you," he said with a wink.

She took a sip of her tea as she continued to watch him. "That makes sense since you normally live at one of your other estates. So do you have one of these cottages on your other properties? Somewhere to take the women you spirit away?"

He leaned back in his chair, arms crossed over his chest, and leveled a direct stare at her. "You are the only woman I've found to be worth the effort."

He spoke with such conviction, no hint of prevarication in his expression. She was sure others would think her foolish, but she believed him. Her throat went dry as he continued to stare at her, and she had to take another sip of her tea before she could continue. "I'm sure every other woman you've wanted fell at your feet."

He didn't move, and she was powerless to look away from him. "I'm no saint, Lily. And many would say I'm no gentleman. But I made sure that any woman who came before you understood that our time together would be brief. I haven't misled anyone."

"Not even me?" Her voice was barely above a whisper.

He winced. "Our whole courtship was a charade. I wanted to sweep you away that first day I met you when you'd come with your sisters to visit Clara in London."

A shiver went through her at the vehemence in his words. "But you didn't."

"No. Instead, I decided that since you were a properly bred young woman, I needed to court you. For the past few months, I've been pretending to be someone I'm not."

She sucked in a breath, shocked that he would admit as much to her. "So all those things you told me… the books you enjoy reading, your love of horses, and… everything." They'd spoken about so much. His plans to improve one of his estates, what he liked to do in his free time.

"Oh, that was all true. But I didn't want to shock you with the strength of how much I wanted you. Not to mention the fact that your father would have barred me from the house if he even suspected."

He drained the rest of his tea, and she couldn't help but wonder if he also found his throat was dry. When she caught herself watching his mouth, remembering how he had kissed her yesterday, she had to force herself to look away.

Everything about this man—his demeanor, the way he looked at her—was so different from the man she'd come to know.

Better, an inner voice said.

She'd liked him well enough before he'd abducted her. Heaven knew the man drew every female eye whenever he walked into a room—hers included. But she'd always had the feeling that he was too polite. Too considerate in how he treated her, if that was even possible. Despite that, she'd yearned for more from him, unable to shake the certainty that there was a side to this man that he wasn't showing her.

She'd feared it was because he didn't actually care for her. That he'd decided to court her because they got along well, and he saw her as a friend who would make an acceptable wife. To learn that Seaford had been hiding just how much he wanted her… Her mouth turned up in a grin as the reality of the situation hit her. She was about to get everything she'd ever wanted. The future she'd been too scared to dream about for fear she'd end up disappointed.

She looked at him again and found he was still watching her. She took a deep breath and spoke the words that would change her life forever. "I want you to show me."

CHAPTER 10

Somehow, Simon kept from jumping out of his chair. He wanted nothing more than to grab this woman and take her upstairs. But this was Lily, and he needed to make sure he wasn't misconstruing her words. There could be no more misunderstandings between them.

"I need to be certain what it is you would like me to show you." When he noticed his hands were actually shaking, he settled them palms down on top of the table and took a steadying breath before continuing. "More kisses?"

She bit her lip and nodded, and he wanted to groan. He didn't think he could touch this woman again and not ravish her.

"Also…"

The word, spoken softly, rocketed through him. "I think you know what it is I want from you. With you. But I need to know that you want it as well."

She took a deep breath and squared her shoulders. "I want you to make love to me."

He didn't leap from the table, not quite, but his chair did scrape against the floor as he pushed it back and stood. Then he stalked around the table—there could be no other word for it—and held his hand out to Lily.

She grasped it without hesitation, and he pulled her up. Then he kissed her.

This time he didn't need to start slowly, nor did he need to keep a respectable distance between their bodies so he wouldn't get carried away. Because this time they wouldn't stop.

He pulled her against him, heat flooding through him at the sensation of this woman's soft body pressed against his harder one, and caught her mouth in a kiss meant to convey just how much he wanted her. As his tongue surged into her warmth, one small part of him urged caution because even though she had consented, Lily was still a maiden.

But it was impossible to heed that warning when Lily opened for him and returned his kiss with equal fervor. Her fingers were in his hair as she held his head close.

Without conscious thought, his hands moved from her waist to her hips and he brought her soft belly against his hardness. If he didn't pull away now, he was going to have this woman right here on the kitchen table, and Lily deserved so much more than that.

Ending their kiss was one of the hardest things he'd ever had to do. He managed it only because he knew this wasn't the end. He bent his knees and swept her into his arms again as he'd done when playing the role of highwayman.

As she did that other time, she grasped him about the neck. But this time, instead of sputtering in indignation, she laughed with joy. That sound had him believing he could do anything in the world.

He carried her upstairs, careful not to bump her into the wall or the banister on the narrow stairs. Which meant, of course, that his back grazed the wall, but he didn't mind. The only thing that mattered right then was Lily.

When they stopped in front of her bedroom door, she reached down to turn the handle. He entered the room and strode to the bed. Then stopped.

He smiled as he looked down at it. "You made the bed?"

"Of course. I don't have a maid here to do it for me. But the sheets aren't tucked in as tightly as they should be." A small vee had formed between her brows at the admission.

He could only shake his head in amusement. He intended to keep the bedsheets in complete disarray over the next few days. How many times would she try to make the bed while he did everything in his power to muss it up again?

He wasn't sure how good the mattress springs were, so he laid her down carefully on top of the smoothed-out linens and stared down at her.

After a few seconds, she squirmed in discomfort. Red tinged her cheeks. "Either you're joining me here or I'm going to stand up right now."

That had him lowering himself to sit on the bed next to her. He took one of her hands and dropped a kiss in the middle of her palm. "I must say you've turned out to be a delightful surprise."

She let out a soft laugh. "I think your impression of *properly bred* young women is entirely too old-fashioned. I can assure you that while many young women may not approve of being kidnapped, we do long to have someone sweep us off our feet."

"And instead, I decided to plod along like a snail."

She tugged him onto the bed next to her. "You made up for it in the end in spectacular fashion."

He'd been off his game for months now, but this he knew how to do. And if he didn't ruin things again, this time they would both be winners.

She brought her hands up to his face, running her thumbs along his cheeks. "I like the way your whiskers feel."

With a grin, he dropped a kiss on her mouth and then brought his face to her neck, where he dragged his stubble against the delicate skin there. He'd have to be careful not to mark her where others might see it after they left the cottage, but he enjoyed the soft sound she made at the rasp of his whiskers against her skin.

Which of course had him thinking of doing the same thing against her breasts and the skin of her inner thighs.

The thought had him hard as a rock, and he took her mouth again. He would have to find the strength to go slow. Not too slow—he'd already learned his lesson there—but he didn't want to go too far in the other direction and scare her away.

He dragged his mouth along her jaw, kissing her just under her ear as he brought his hands to her waist. When she clasped him about the shoulders, her eager movements telling him that she enjoyed what he was doing to her, he cupped her breasts.

Her gasp of pleasure echoed his own groan. He stared down at her, enjoying the way her head was thrown back, her lower lip held between her teeth.

He traced her nipples. "Are you fine with me touching you here?"

She nodded, and he tugged down the bodice of her gown. Her eyes flew open, but she didn't protest.

Thank the heavens that she wasn't wearing stays. He palmed her through her chemise and then dropped his head to draw one rosy tip into his mouth through the fabric.

Her hands had moved to the back of his head and she held him in place.

As though he would ever want to be anywhere else.

He pushed her onto her back and switched his attention to the other breast. Emboldened by her enjoyment, he pulled down her chemise and then brought her soft breast into his mouth.

His blood heated at the small gasps of pleasure that escaped her throat. These weren't the practiced moans of a woman who was playing a role for him. He'd always taken great care when seeing to a woman's pleasure before taking his own, but he'd be a fool not to know that many of those women went to almost comical lengths to show their appreciation.

But not Lily. Her gasps were soft, as though she was surprised but nonetheless delighted by the fact she was enjoying his attention very much. There was nothing false or exaggerated about her cries.

Which had him aching to bring her to heights she could never have imagined.

He lifted his head and hovered over her. He knew this would end in him taking her maidenhead, but before that happened, he needed her to find release. He wasn't sure if she'd be able to do that with him inside her this first time.

She opened her eyes, and they stared at one another.

"Are we going to make love now?" Her voice was lower than normal, husky from her passion.

"Soon, my love. But first I need to prepare you. Your first time will hurt."

She licked her lips. "I know."

He kissed her and used one hand to drag up the skirts of her dress. She gasped into his mouth when he skimmed a hand along the delicate skin of her inner thigh, but she didn't stop him. When he reached that sweet place between her thighs, she shifted her head to one side and clenched her jaw.

He stilled. "Am I hurting you?"

She shook her head. "I'm getting ready for the pain."

He chuckled. "Not yet, Lily. First there is only pleasure."

She was so wet, and he couldn't wait to make this woman his. She let out a shuddering breath when he entered her with one finger, but the sound turned into another moan of enjoyment when he began to tease the sensitive bundle of nerves at the top of her opening with his thumb.

She bit her bottom lip again, and he was mesmerized as he watched the expressions that crossed her face. Every muscle in his body was stretched taut as he continued to concentrate all his attention on her pleasure, using his other hand to play with her sensitive breasts. But he kept his gaze riveted on her face, wanting to ensure he wasn't hurting her.

He didn't have to wait long before her hands tightened on his upper arms. She called out his name, and then the most glorious expression crossed her face as her release swept through her.

He stilled, then removed his hand and braced himself over her. Lily's eyes were wide with wonder.

"I never imagined…" She shook her head. "I was told that lovemaking could be a wondrous experience, but I never thought I'd enjoy it that much."

Her hand cupped his cheek, and he kissed her again. This time he kept his movements slow and languorous, needing to cool his own raging desire. He wanted to sink into Lily and claim her forever, but it troubled him to know he would cause her pain.

"If you want to wait—"

She moved her hand to cover his mouth. "No more waiting."

He licked her hand, and she removed it with a giggle.

"You're ticklish," he said.

She frowned at him. "No."

He laughed and flipped their positions so that

she was lying on him. "I'll have to use that information to my advantage later. But for now, there's something else we need to do."

She lowered her head to kiss him but froze when a loud thumping came from downstairs.

Damn it. Someone was knocking on the front door.

CHAPTER 11

The pounding of fists on the front door downstairs had the same effect as someone standing over them and throwing a basin of water onto their heated bodies.

Lily froze for several seconds as her mind tried to process what she was hearing. "Someone is here," she said in a whisper.

"They're outside." Seaford rose from the bed.

Lily scrambled up as well, pulling her chemise and dress back into place. Seaford was still fully clothed. The only sign they'd been engaged in intimacies was his hair, which was now tousled from her fingers raking through it. She knew the same couldn't be said for her.

"I'm sure it's Hastings. He must need to speak to me. I'll go see what he wants."

She nodded as she flew to the small dressing table and glanced at the mirror. Seaford had taken her hair down with only a few swift flicks of his fingers. She tried not to dwell on what that said about his experience undressing women. As for his other actions… well, if she had any doubts before, it was clear this man was no saint. Which gave credence to his assertion he'd been going out of his way to behave as a proper gentleman when he was courting her. Because it was now clear that the Earl of Seaford was not lacking in passion.

She set about twisting her hair and pinning it back onto her head. She heard the unmistakable sound of the front door opening and then the soft murmur of male voices. She took comfort in the fact that their voices weren't raised. She'd been half afraid her father had learned about Seaford's actions and had set out to track them down.

When Seaford returned a few minutes later, she was sitting on the edge of the bed. She'd managed to calm her racing heart, but her body still thrummed with heat and desire for this man. She said nothing as he crossed the room and lowered himself onto the bed next to her.

"I apologize for the interruption."

Lily winced. "It takes a little of the romance out of the situation when I'm reminded that others know we're here together and no doubt imagining what we're doing."

"Hastings will never reveal what he knows."

Lily examined his features for a hint of uncertainty, but she could see none.

"But he did come with news," he said.

Lily's breath caught. "Does Father know about us? Or perhaps something has happened to Iris or Violet—"

He cut her off with a kiss that lasted longer than it should have. It was unseemly how easily this man could distract her.

He pulled back and gazed down at her.

"Nothing like that. But your father is worried about you traveling alone. He sent a note."

She hadn't even noticed that he had a letter in his hand until he held it out to her.

She took it and broke the seal, surprised that her fingers weren't shaking. Her eyes skimmed over the page. It was just as Seaford had said—a few lines about how he was writing to make sure that she'd arrived at the Thornton estate safely. He also wanted to make sure she wasn't feeling lonely being apart from her family.

Lily almost laughed aloud at that. Seaford hadn't given her the opportunity to think about anyone but him. "Father is waiting for my reply."

Seaford nodded. "Hastings is downstairs. He took the liberty of bringing everything you'd need to write a letter."

Lily rose to her feet, her thoughts whirling as she went to the window and looked outside. Behind her, Seaford stood and she knew he was watching her. Waiting for her reply.

"I can't lie to my father."

"You wouldn't have to. You did arrive at your destination safely. And I imagine it wouldn't be a falsehood to tell him you're enjoying yourself."

She turned and smiled at him. "I am, so very much. But I need to return."

He let out a breath and closed the distance between them. "I expected you to say as much."

"Are you going to keep me here anyway?"

His brows drew together in a slight frown. "Of course not. I've already told you that I won't force you to do anything. If you wish to return to the estate, we'll do that."

She winced. "We can't return together. I must

go alone. Did your valet bring the carriage? I can leave with him now." She turned back to look at her reflection in the mirror again. "I should probably change first. My dress is a little rumpled after this morning's activities."

Heat rose to her cheeks, but she couldn't regret what had happened between them. Her only disappointment was that their time together had been so short.

Her thoughts flitted from one thing to the next as she tried to settle on what she needed to do first. What was she going to say when she returned? Seaford would want her to lie to her father about what had happened.

His large hands settled on her shoulders. She met his gaze in the dressing table mirror as he drew her back against his chest. "Breathe, Lily. We have time to talk about what is going to happen next."

He was correct. She closed her eyes and leaned back into him. When his arms wrapped around her waist, she put her own arms over them. She took comfort from the way he surrounded her body, holding her in a protective embrace.

She took several deep breaths and willed her nerves to settle. Everything would be fine. Seaford had planned this adventure with great care. So of course he would have made plans for what would come next.

A few minutes passed like that, Seaford's warmth wrapping around her. When she opened her eyes, he was watching her in the mirror. "What do we do now?"

He dropped a kiss into her hair. "You're correct that you need to change. Then I'll help you pack your belongings while Hastings fetches the carriage. He left it a little ways down the road."

She took a deep breath and nodded.

"But before we do anything else, I have something to ask you."

He removed his arms from around her waist and turned her to face him. Then he dropped to one knee.

"Lily Rowland, you've led me on a merry chase. I fumbled things badly the first time I asked, but you should know that my feelings are unchanged. Please make me the happiest of men and say that you'll agree to be my wife."

Warmth unfurled in her chest. Had it only been one week since she'd turned down this man's proposal of marriage? She'd been a fool. She opened her mouth to reply, but he held up one finger to stop her.

"You should know that I promise to fill every one of your days—and your nights—with more passion than you can imagine."

She laughed. "I'm not sure that's possible. I've been told that I have a very vivid imagination."

One corner of his mouth kicked up in a wicked grin, and her heart did a little flip in her chest. She would never get used to just how handsome this man was—and soon he was going to be hers.

"If you accept me, I'm sure I'll be up to the challenge. But I don't think I'll be able to successfully abduct you a second time if you refuse me."

She reached for his hands and tugged him back to his feet. She could only stare at him, unable to believe she'd gained this man's attention.

After several seconds, he brought her hands to his mouth and dropped a kiss onto each of her palms. "You haven't answered me."

She smiled. "No, I haven't."

His brows drew together. "I love you, Lily, and I won't give up. But I don't think I could handle another rejection from you."

Her mouth dropped open, shock rippling through her, and she had to snap it closed. "You love me?"

His brow furrowed. "Of course I do. Why would I go to all this trouble if I didn't love you?"

She gazed up at him in wonder. "I love you too. And yes, I'll marry you."

He kissed her then, quickly, and reached into a small pocket on his waistcoat. He pulled out an ornate gold ring. If she wasn't mistaken, it held a large ruby surrounded by small diamonds. "This was my parents' betrothal ring. If it doesn't fit, I can have it resized for you."

She sucked in a breath. "You didn't have this the last time you asked me."

He shook his head. "I did. I've been carrying it around with me for some time. I just didn't have the chance to give it to you the first time I proposed."

What was he saying? "You've had this the whole time?"

"I hoped you'd give me another chance to ask you again."

She placed a hand over the small pocket that was on the left side of his waistcoat, then dragged her hand to the center of his chest. "Close to your heart." Her voice was low, the significance of his actions speaking volumes.

"It's where you've been since I met you." He slid the ring onto her finger, and she was pleased to see that it fit her perfectly. As though it had been made for her.

He gathered her into his arms, and they stayed like that for several minutes. She wanted to remain there forever. Finally, far too soon for her liking, he dropped another kiss on top of her head and pulled back to look down at her. "I've already given some thought about what we're going to tell your family."

She winced at the reminder. "We can't tell them you kidnapped me and whisked me away to your secret lair."

"No. But I don't expect you to lie. To begin, we'll return together. When we arrive at the estate, I'll take your father aside. I'll tell him that I went to see you at the Thornton's house party and was able to convince you to change your mind."

It was a believable fabrication. Far more believable than the truth. And given that her father was unlikely to ask his niece and her husband for any of the details about their Christmas house party, he wouldn't learn she'd never been there.

"Perhaps I should return on my own first——"

He dropped a kiss onto her lips. "No. I'm not letting you out of my sight. Not until I've had your father's agreement and everyone knows you'll soon be the next Countess of Seaford."

"You need have no fear about that. Father might even cease being angry with me for denying you the first time."

"I was less than pleased myself, but in retrospect…" He shook his head.

She frowned. "Surely you're not glad that I refused you?"

He lifted one shoulder in a shrug. "Who knows how much longer I would have carried on pretending to be a proper suitor?" He shuddered. "And we never would have had this delightful little adventure."

"That's true," she said. She was about to say more but embarrassment had her holding her tongue.

Seaford must have seen her hesitation. "What are you thinking?"

She covered her face with her hands. After the intimacies they'd already shared, she really shouldn't be so shy around this man. Dropping her hands, she met his gaze. "That it would have been nice if your servant could have waited another few hours before delivering his message."

He pulled her against him, and she felt his hardness press into her belly. Regret filled her as she wondered whether they'd have another opportunity to be alone together before they wed.

"Make no mistake," he said into her hair. "We'll be getting to that very soon." Then he released her. "I need to go now while I still can."

With that, he strode from the room, closing the door carefully behind him.

Lily stared at the door for a few seconds and then spun in a circle, her eyes closed as she allowed pure joy to bubble through her.

Seaford loved her. It was true that they were still friends—she hadn't been wrong about that—but they were also so much more.

When she'd woken yesterday morning, the future appeared bleak. Now it promised to hold far more happiness than she could have imagined.

CHAPTER 12

Simon was relieved Lily had managed to rein in her panic after reading her father's note. Hopefully she'd be able to dress herself because he wasn't sure he'd be able to help her. Not when he wanted to do the exact opposite.

He summoned Hastings to his room to help him with his own preparations. When they arrived at his estate together, it couldn't be obvious that he'd just left Lily's bed. He needed to behave with the propriety her father expected from him.

Even if the only thing Simon wanted to do was swing the man's daughter over his shoulder and carry her to his bedroom so they could finish what they'd started.

But it seemed the fates were conspiring against him, and he'd have to wait. Again.

He took the seat next to Lily in the carriage, his heart soaring when she'd allowed him to put his arm around her and draw her to his side. Hastings had already brought his mount back to the estate last night, so he was saved from having to ride outside where he would have spent the entire trip fretting about how Lily was faring inside the carriage.

Her head rested against his shoulder, her eyes closed. But he knew Lily wasn't asleep. She would be thinking about the scandalous fact they were returning together. Unchaperoned and unwed.

He dropped a kiss into her hair. "Try not to fret. Everything will work out as it should."

They stayed like that for the half-hour trip back. When the carriage began to slow, she looked up at him, her eyes wide.

He stole a kiss from her delectable lips and then moved to the opposite bench. He knew it wasn't enough. Her father would still worry about what had happened in that carriage, especially since they were supposed to be returning from the Thornton house party, but he wouldn't flaunt their indiscretions. Not when he hoped to repeat them soon.

"Your father will be happy for us," he said.

Lily sighed. "I know. But I'm not looking forward to the lecture he'll deliver when he pulls me aside."

He should be feeling guilty about causing this woman even a moment of trouble, but he didn't. He'd do everything all over again. It had only given them one day together, but he'd achieved his goal of winning Lily's heart.

They'd discussed what would happen next. When the carriage arrived, he expected everyone's curiosity would have them coming to see who was in it.

So when he opened the carriage door and stepped down, he wasn't surprised to find their families spilling from the house to stand by the entrance. He gave Lily a reassuring smile as he helped her down from the carriage.

The group remained close to the house, not wanting to step farther out into the cold. His sister was whispering with Lily's sisters, smiles and giggles making it clear that their hopes for a wedding had been restored.

His mother gave him a chiding look as she welcomed them back, but he could tell she was doing everything in her power to hide how much she enjoyed seeing the two of them together. When he turned to look at Lily's father, he couldn't discern what the man was thinking.

"I'm so happy to see the two of you here," his mother said as everyone moved into the house. "But you must tell us how the two of you came to arrive here together."

"Yes," Mr. Rowland said, his brows drawing together. "Please share how you came to be alone in a carriage with my daughter when I was told you'd returned to London."

The hint of anger in the man's tone wasn't surprising. Seaford had expected much more.

"Of course. But first I must speak to Mr. Rowland alone."

That had their sisters gasping and then whispering again. He was relieved to see that Lily was the picture of calm.

He led her father to his study and closed the door behind them.

"I don't want to know the details," Rowland said. "Just tell me that you've managed to convince my stubborn daughter to accept your suit."

Seaford managed not to grin. "I did."

Rowland nodded. "And this happened at Thornton's Christmas party?"

He inclined his head. The lie was a necessary one, and he knew that Lily's father wouldn't go out of his way to confirm it. As Rowland had already said, he didn't want to know exactly what had happened.

"Good. I take it you'll be getting a special license?"

"I plan to leave for London first thing in the morning."

It was a week before Christmas. He'd have to call in some favors, but he was certain he could get the license this close to the holiday.

And then he'd finally have Lily, which was the best Christmas gift he could have asked for.

HE FOUND IT DIFFICULT TO HOLD ON TO HIS optimism as the day progressed. Whenever he thought he'd be able to snatch a moment alone with Lily, one of their sisters would intrude and pull her aside to join them in some activity or other. And while his mother would have looked away to allow them a few minutes together, Lily's father was not of the same mind.

Finally he gave up and headed to his study. He

didn't need anyone to tell him he'd been mooning after her like a lovesick fool. No one said as much, but he had the impression their sisters were taking an inordinate amount of pleasure in ensuring he and Lily were kept apart.

Perhaps it was what he deserved after making Lily feel that she wasn't welcome here, but he'd had enough of the glances and giggles that were aimed his way.

He tried to go over the account books, but he couldn't concentrate on numbers. Then he tried reading, but his thoughts kept straying to that morning's passionate encounter and the fact that Lily wasn't his yet.

He was pacing when a brisk knock at the study door sounded a moment before it was flung open. Clara stormed into the room and stopped in front of him. She settled her hands on her hips and scowled at him.

He let out a sigh. He didn't know why his sister was so angry with him. He was the one being thwarted at every turn. "You wished to speak to me?"

"I am very cross with you. Violet just told me that you'd already asked for Lily's hand, and you never said a word about it. And then you bungled it badly, and she refused you!"

He reached up to rub at the back of his neck, where the tension of the day had settled like a knot. "I didn't want to disappoint you and Mother."

She stamped her foot, and he had to force himself not to roll his eyes at her dramatics. "I could have helped you," she said, flinging her arms wide. "Spoken to her and tried to get her to see that you're not all that bad."

He let out a dry chuckle. "That's high praise indeed coming from you. I'm sure she would have flung herself into my arms and accepted me on the spot after learning I wasn't *all that bad.*"

"Simon." His name was a drawn-out whine.

"I already had a plan and didn't want to involve you. I would make a poor prospect for a husband if I needed to have my little sister beg a woman to accept my suit."

She crossed her arms over her chest. "I'm sixteen."

He raised one brow. "Your point?"

She let out a huff in annoyance. "Your *plan* is the other reason I'm angry with you. Why did you have to seek her out and propose again at the

Thornton's house party? You could have done it here."

He smiled. He and Lily had only spent one day together in that small cottage, but he'd always cherish the memories they'd made there. In fact, he'd make sure to visit again after they wed. Finish what had so unceremoniously been interrupted.

Clara let out an impatient huff. Then she threw herself at him and wrapped her arms around his waist. "I'm so glad you were able to fix things even if I don't approve of being kept in the dark. Lily, Iris, and Violet are like sisters to me. And now they'll be family."

He hugged her. "I'll admit I'm also relieved. Miss Rowland had me worried for a bit."

Clara pulled away. "You're forgiven. Now come along. It's almost dinner, and you shouldn't be buried away in your study. After, we're going to the music room and will take turns playing and singing. It will be so much fun. But you have to promise not to join in. We don't need your horrible singing voice ruining what will be a fun evening."

He could only shake his head as he followed Clara from the room, trying to push away the frustration that gnawed at him. He'd waited this long for Lily Rowland. Surely one more evening wouldn't kill him.

HE WAS WRONG... THE EVENING WAS GOING TO DO him in. Watching Lily as she laughed and smiled at everyone. Listening to her sing while their sisters played the pianoforte, her sweet voice wrapping around him. And the twinkle in her eyes whenever she glanced at him had him wanting to spirit her away from the room.

But her father was guarding her like a hawk. She couldn't even sit next to him, in a room filled with people, without Rowland glaring at him and inching closer so they couldn't have a private conversation.

Not that Lily's father was wrong in distrusting him. But Simon was going to be leaving for London in the morning, and he wanted at least a few minutes alone with his betrothed before then.

Finally the last song was played and the evening's entertainments were finished. Much laughter and hugs were shared as everyone said their good-nights and made their way from the room. And then it was just the three of them. Him, Lily, and Lily's father.

Rowland moved to the doorway but didn't leave. Simon wanted to growl at the man, but Lily's hand on his arm made him realize he was scowling.

"You're leaving in the morning?" she asked.

He had to keep his hands clasped behind his back so he wouldn't reach for her and drag her into his arms. He didn't care that it would anger Rowland. He was going to marry this woman, after all, and the man was unlikely to forbid the match at this late stage.

Still, he knew that angering her father would upset Lily, and that knowledge was enough to keep him on his best behavior.

"I'll be off to London for a special license. After waiting six months and having you turn me down once, I find I no longer have the patience to wait."

She smiled at him. "I agree."

She started to lean closer, and before he could reach for her and give her the kiss she clearly wanted, Lily's father was at her side. With a sigh, she waved at him over her shoulder as Rowland dragged her away.

He regretted not spiriting Lily away to Gretna Green while he had the chance.

Frustration had him stalking to his bedroom. Perhaps all was not lost. If Hastings didn't already know, he could ask the man to make discrete inquiries about where Lily was sleeping. Then, after a suitable amount of time had passed, Simon could make his way to Lily's bedroom.

His mother waylaid him for a few minutes, telling him how happy she was that he had made up with Lily. Like his sister, she also chastised him for making Lily feel as though she wasn't welcome there.

When he finally reached his bedroom, he wasn't surprised to find Hastings was already there. This man had been invaluable to him over the past week.

"Do you know where Miss Rowland is sleeping tonight?"

His valet inclined his head. "Of course. There is little that goes on under this roof that I don't know."

Simon blew out a breath. "Good. How long should I wait before I can safely make my way there?"

"It goes without saying that now would be too soon."

He frowned at the man. He knew that Hastings was trying to ease his employer's tension with humor, but the only thing Simon needed was Lily in his arms again.

Hastings bounced on his feet, and Simon didn't hold back his groan. If his valet was excited, it must mean that Hastings had ordered new clothes for him and wanted to test their fit. Simon was in no mood to indulge the man even if he did owe him a debt. "I'm not changing."

The corners of his valet's mouth turned up ever so slightly. "I do think you should look in your dressing room. I've recently *acquired* something that I think will be of great interest to you."

Simon pulled out his pocket watch and took in the time. How much longer would he have to wait before he could safely sneak through the house to his betrothed's bedroom? Perhaps it would be better to allow Hastings to dress him up in another outfit. It would allow some of that time to pass.

He turned and crossed to his dressing room. His hand was on the doorknob when he heard his bedroom door open and close. When he turned, he found he was alone in the room.

Wondering just what Hastings was playing at, he continued into the dressing room.

And found Lily standing there, waiting for him.

"I hope I'm not intruding on your personal time."

The grin that crossed Seaford's face made her glad she'd risked coming here. She'd dismissed the maid soon after her father had deposited her at the bedroom door, telling her she wouldn't be needed. Impatience had her risking exposure, but when she'd slipped out of her bedroom, the earl's valet was waiting for her in the hallway.

She hadn't asked if the earl had sent for her or if he'd somehow read her mind and known she meant to find her way to the room Clara had once mentioned belonged to her brother. She'd allowed him to lead her here and had been amused when he'd asked her to wait in the dressing room.

Seaford opened his arms, and she threw herself at him. She loved her family and appreciated the way Clara had gone out of her way to make Lily feel as though they were already sisters. But as the hours passed and it became clear she wouldn't have another moment alone with this man, she'd known it was time to take matters into her own hands. To show Seaford that she too was willing to take a risk for him. For them.

He gave his head a small shake. "I can't believe you came here. I was doing everything in my power not to march straight to your bedroom while there was still a risk I'd be seen."

"Alas, I've never been known for my patience," she said with an exaggerated sigh. "And I didn't want to risk not seeing you again before you had to leave."

He lowered his head until his mouth hovered over hers. "That was never going to happen."

And then he kissed her, and she forgot about everything and everyone except for this man who would soon be her husband.

She let out a gasp when he swung her into his arms. "You need to warn me before you do that. I could have screamed."

He grinned down at her. "You still might."

Then he carried her from the dressing room and lowered her onto his bed. "But first, I need to lock the door so we won't be interrupted again."

She laughed. "I've already warned Mr. Hastings."

HE COULD ONLY SHAKE HIS HEAD IN SURPRISE AS HE moved to the door. It seemed that Lily had lost some of her inhibitions. He'd have to see what he could do about causing her to drop the ones that remained.

When he turned back to her, his hand was already loosening his cravat. He enjoyed the way her eyes widened as he pulled the fabric from his throat, allowing his shirt to drop open at the neck.

He made quick work of removing his waistcoat and then drew his shirt up over his head. Lily's eyes remained fixed on him the whole time, although now they lowered to his chest. When her tongue dipped out to lick her lower lip, he couldn't hold back his groan.

He made quick work of his trousers and then lowered himself to lie next to her.

Only now Lily was sitting up, her gaze traveling

up and down his body before snagging on his hard length.

"I think I'm wearing too much," she said finally.

He laughed and stretched out to allow her to look her fill. "I can lie here and watch you disrobe."

She shook her head and covered her face with her hands. "I don't think I'm ready for that. Not yet."

He would hold her to that unspoken promise, but he could work with what he had. "Kiss me, Lily."

She peeked at him through her fingers before finally dropping her hands. She took a breath, gathering her courage, and then leaned forward. When her hands remained on her lap, he laughed.

"You can touch me."

She shook her head. "I feel ridiculous."

"Never," he said, taking hold of her hands and bringing them to his chest.

Her mouth dropped open for a moment before her lips curved into a smile. Then she was exploring his chest, his shoulders, his arms. When she brought them back to his chest, she kissed him.

He tugged her down, and her breath came out in another gasp as he dragged her over his body. She let out a soft moan as he deepened the kiss, giving her a small taste of just how he wanted to devour her.

His patience at an end, he pulled down the bodice of her dress so her breasts could spring free. He rolled so she was now under him and devoured her soft flesh. Her fingers combed through his hair as she held him against her.

"You make me feel things I never imagined possible," she said, her voice ragged with desire.

He stared down at her, taking a few moments to regain control. This was her first time and it would hurt, but damn, he wanted to be inside her so much he might just die from the pressure building within him.

He'd wanted to strip her dress from her delightful body so she was as naked as him, but that would come next time. For now, he shifted onto one elbow and inched up her skirts.

"That's it," he said when she opened her legs for him.

Like last time, he used his fingers to bring her to her first orgasm. And when her body was still spasming around his fingers, her lower lip clenched between her teeth to hold back her cries, he moved into position. Ever so slowly, he inched his way into her warm, welcoming body.

Her soft gasp told him that he'd breached her maidenhead, but he didn't stop until he was seated fully within her.

It was almost impossible not to keep going. He tried counting in his head, telling himself she needed time to adjust to his invasion. He'd reached twenty when Lily shifted.

"I thought there would be more," she said.

He couldn't hold back a chuckle. By way of reply, he pulled out of her body then eased himself back in. His eyes remained fixed on her face, watching for any sign that he was hurting her.

Her soft "oh" of astonishment told him everything he needed to know. He began to move slowly then, spurred on by the way she wrapped her legs around him and arched up into his body. He had never wanted to be with a woman more than Lily, and now that he finally had her, he never wanted their time together to stop.

When she came apart, her mouth pressed against his shoulder to muffle her screams, he was right behind her.

He kissed her as his length softened inside her, and then he turned so they were on their sides, facing one another.

She reached out to twine the fingers of one

hand with his. "I can see now why Celia enjoys being with her husband so much."

He squeezed her fingers. "I hate that I must leave you tomorrow."

A small vee formed between her brows. "Must you go so soon?"

"The sooner I go, the sooner we can wed. And then nothing will keep us apart. But for now"—he rolled onto his back, and Lily nestled into his side—"we can spend some time together."

Her body needed time to heal before they could make love again, but he could at least hold her until it was time for her to return to her bedroom.

CHAPTER 14

Surely an eternity had passed since Lily had last seen Seaford. Five days. She couldn't hold back her fear that it would begin to snow and the roads would become impassable. A special license would do them no good if her betrothed couldn't reach her.

They'd said their goodbyes to Clara and Lady Seaford yesterday and were now back home. Father was the only person happy about that situation.

Seaford's mother had extended an invitation to have them stay until Christmas. Violet and Iris had tried to cajole Father to accept, but his mind wouldn't be swayed. Lily had known the effort would be futile.

Perhaps next year, when she was the new countess, they could all spend Christmas there.

Lily stood and walked over to the windows of the morning room. It was midmorning, and as was their custom, they were passing the time with various activities. Violet was scribbling away in her journal, and Iris was working on a drawing.

Lily had been trying to read. She peered out the window into their back garden. "Do you think it will snow?"

Violet let out an exasperated sigh. "Since neither one of us can predict the future, why do you insist on asking that same question twenty times a day?"

"Just twenty?" Iris said. "I'd say that number is closer to fifty."

Lily blew out a breath. Then she spotted a lone snowflake drifting on the wind, and her heart threatened to stop. She snatched up her book. "I'm going to take this to the drawing room." Where she'd be able to see an approaching horse.

"He's not going to get here any faster if you stare out a different window," Iris said.

Lily ignored her and was just about to leave the room when a knock at the front door echoed through the house. Lily dropped her book on a chair and raced down the hall, reaching the door just as the butler did.

She held her breath and waited for the man to open the door.

When it did, Seaford was standing on the threshold.

Somehow she restrained herself from pushing past their butler and throwing herself into his arms. Aware of voices behind her, she aimed for a level tone as she took a step closer. "You took longer than I expected."

His gaze was intense, and she knew, from the heat reflected in his eyes, that he was remembering the night they'd spent together.

"I reached the estate last night. Mother said she was going to ask you to stay. Imagine my disappointment when I discovered you'd all gone home."

"Are the two of you going to stand in the doorway all day?" Father said from behind her.

Lily laughed and stepped aside with an apology. She waited while Seaford handed his winter garments to the butler and was rewarded with a kiss to her cheek.

He moved to whisper into her ear. "Soon we'll be able to do much more than that."

"Not in Father's presence. I don't think he'll care how long we've been married."

Seaford raised a brow at that but said nothing, and she had the impression that he'd taken her words as a challenge. She still forgot, on occasion, that he wasn't the politely distant man who had courted her.

He tucked her hand into his arm, and together they entered the drawing room. Three sets of eyes were fixed on them.

"Well, don't keep us waiting," Father said. "Did you get what you were after?"

Seaford inclined his head, and Lily's heart lightened with relief.

He turned to her. "I took the liberty of stopping by your parish church and had a pleasant conversation with Mr. Bailey. He's agreed to marry us this afternoon."

Lily's hands flew to cover her mouth, which was gaping open most unbecomingly. "So soon?"

"Soon? We've been courting for months now."

"Your mother and your sister—"

"Are on their way. I didn't want to wait for them to get ready, so I rode on ahead."

"But—"

He placed one finger on her lips. "Have you changed your mind?"

She searched his gaze and saw that he was genuinely concerned. Of course he was. She'd already turned down his proposal once.

His finger was still on her mouth, and so she clasped his hand between hers. She dropped a kiss onto the center of his palm and then lowered it.

"Never." She let out a soft laugh of disbelief. "It appears we're getting married today. I can just imagine the rumors that will spread at our haste."

Father cleared his throat, and she dropped Seaford's hand and took a step back.

Her sisters swept forward to engulf Lily in a hug.

"At least now you won't need to spend the entire day staring out the window waiting for Lord Seaford," Violet said in a whisper that everyone in the room could hear.

Lily wasn't even embarrassed. She was far too happy for any other emotion to take up room in her heart.

"Shush," Iris said. "We're going to let the maid know that she'll be needed soon." She gave Lord Seaford a small curtsy and then dragged Violet from the room.

Lily turned to face her father. "Can I speak to Lord Seaford for a moment?"

She almost expected him to say no. Instead, he drew her into a hug. "I love you, Lily. I'm pleased this day has come."

She pulled back to stare up at him, shocked that one tear was tracing down his cheek. "I love you too, Father."

He gave his head a shake and let out a breath. "That's enough of this sentimental nonsense. We need to get the two of you married. Heaven knows this man must have the patience of a saint to have waited all this time." He shook his head again. "And Thornton told me to keep an eye on you because you were a rake."

With a silent laugh he strode from the room.

Words failed her. She stared after her father for several seconds then turned to see the scowl on Seaford's face.

"I'm going to have a few words with Thornton."

Lily stood on tiptoes and pressed a kiss onto his cheek. Seaford's arms wrapped around her as he brought her closer.

"I've missed you," she said. "Our time together was far too short."

He raised a brow. "Six months, Lily. Six months being on my best behavior when all I wanted to do was spirit you away and have my wicked way with you."

A shiver of anticipation raced down her spine. "You'll have me tonight and every night after that."

"Don't forget the days. I wouldn't want you to accuse me again of lacking in passion."

The gleam in his eyes told her she'd never have to worry about that happening.

EPILOGUE

Two days before Christmas

They were a small yet boisterous group as they spilled from the small parish church that afternoon.

Lily was tugged away from her new husband by Iris, Violet, and Clara, who engulfed her in hugs.

Seaford's mother smiled fondly before pulling her into an embrace as well. "You're good for him," she said into Lily's ear. "I'm very happy to welcome you into the family."

Father cleared his throat. "We should all return home for a pre-Christmas/very late wedding breakfast."

They all erupted into laughter, and Lily gave him a hug. "Thank you."

When the maid had helped her dress, she'd chattered nonstop about how Mr. Rowland had put the staff on alert, telling them that they were to prepare to have the wedding breakfast on a moment's notice.

Lily looked over to the side, where Seaford was speaking to his sister and mother. When Lady Seaford's hand flew to her mouth, Lily made a note to ask him what he'd said. Whatever it was, it had Clara giving her brother an exuberant hug.

Her sisters were saying something to her, but Lily could only hear her heart thundering in her ears as Seaford turned his head and met her gaze. There was an intensity in his expression that had her thinking she needed to look away for the sake of propriety.

She hoped that Mr. Bailey hadn't followed them out because her husband's wicked thoughts were laid bare on his face for the world to see. Her sisters may not understand what that look meant, but her father would.

Seaford strode across the few feet that separated them and then swung her into his arms. She gasped with shock and wrapped her arms around his neck. Her cheeks heated with color.

"What are you doing?" she hissed under her breath. "Surely you could have waited until later. What will everyone say?"

His grin was full of wicked promise as he turned and strode toward the two carriages they'd taken to the church. "They'll say that I didn't have the decency to wait until after the wedding breakfast, but instead carried you off to my lair with unseemly haste."

Her mouth dropped open before she snapped it closed again. "What… lair?"

"Yes, my love. I'm abducting you. And I have the perfect little cottage waiting for us."

"But our families "

He dropped a kiss onto her mouth. "My mother and sister know not to expect us. I have other plans for you."

And that was how Lily Rowland, now the new Countess of Seaford, was said to have received a highwayman for Christmas that year.

I HOPE YOU ENJOYED READING LILY AND SIMON'S story. Iris Rowland's Christmas scandal will be coming next year! To learn when it becomes available, sign up for my newsletter here.

SNEAK PEEK OF THE UNWILLING VISCOUNT

Turn the page to read an excerpt of the latest release in my LANDING A LORD series, *The Unwilling Viscount*. If you like pretend courtships, masquerades, spinster heroines or friends-to-lovers stories, you won't want to miss it!

EXCERPT – THE UNWILLING VISCOUNT

The Viscount Ashford has no immediate plans to wed. But with a mother determined to see him settled by the end of the Season, he must do what he can to salvage his freedom. Which leaves him with one choice—convince Miss Mary Trenton to accept his pretend suit. The woman he's come to think of as a friend is impervious to his charms, and that makes her the perfect choice for this pretend courtship.

Mary has no illusions that Ashford would look twice at her under normal circumstances. Agreeing to help him will allow her to experience what it is like to have a man pursue her. But somewhere along the way, while enjoying the gossip they're stirring, the line between fiction and reality becomes blurred.

Is it possible the attraction she's feeling for Ashford might be reciprocated?

Viscount Ashford stood before his Mayfair town house and stared at the front door for almost a full minute. Dread settled over him at the thought of what awaited him on the other side of that door.

His mother.

She'd sent him a note last week to inform him she was coming to town for the season and that she intended to stay with him. He could only hope she didn't expect him to escort her to all the various entertainments.

The house had remained empty after his father's death several years ago, and he'd taken up residence last summer after returning to England following his time in the army. His mother normally stayed with one of his sisters when she was in town, but both Jane and Helen were now married and had households of their own.

He squared his shoulders and took a deep,

calming breath. He'd faced his share of foes across the battlefield. Surely he could handle having his petite mother in residence for a few months.

The butler opened the door as soon as Ashford reached it. If Hastings had seen him hesitating outside the house, he gave no indication.

It was early evening, and he assumed his mother would be resting before dinner as was her custom. "Is Lady Ashford in her chambers?"

Hastings inclined his head. "Yes, my lord. Lady Benington is also here. She's waiting for you in the library."

Of course she was. Jane wouldn't miss the spectacle that was about to take place. At least his youngest sister, Helen, wasn't in town this spring. He was only slightly outnumbered.

He thanked the man and headed down the hallway to the library. He was delaying what he knew would be an uncomfortable meeting with his mother, but his sister would always be the lesser of two evils.

When he reached the room, Jane was standing near the window, looking out onto the back garden.

She turned as he entered, and one corner of her mouth quirked up in amusement. "I half feared you'd quit London. I'm happy to see Mother hasn't succeeded in driving you away. Not yet at any rate."

He fought to hold back a scowl as he waited for her to settle into a chair and then sank into the seat opposite her. As always, his sister was exquisitely dressed, and he didn't even have to ask if she'd be joining them for dinner. She wore a deep blue formal dress, and her light brown hair had been styled into ringlets around her face. Small blue jewels were sprinkled throughout the mass, which was swept up in an artful manner. If she planned to cajole him into accompanying her to a ball or rout that evening, she would be disappointed.

"Please tell me you're here to convince Mother to spend the next few months with you."

Jane let out a light laugh. "I'm already wed and have given her two grandchildren. Mother doesn't care what I do with my time. She's more interested in you and your pursuits."

He frowned. "If she's hoping one of those pursuits will be a wife, she's doomed to disappointment." It wasn't that he never wanted to wed, but it wasn't something he planned to do in the near future. When he married, it would be when he decided it was time.

"I don't know about that. Mother can be quite determined when she puts her mind to something."

He'd seen a hint of that strength the previous year when he'd visited her after resigning his commission and returning to England. Still, she couldn't have changed that much. The woman he'd known when he was a youth had deferred to her husband in all things.

"If she becomes unbearable, I'll find somewhere else to stay." He could just imagine the look on Lowenbrock's or Cranston's face if he turned up at one of their houses and asked them for shelter. He'd never hear the end of it, but they'd never abandon him in his hour of need.

"That won't dissuade our mother from carrying out her mission."

He let out a soft chuckle at the thought. "Are we talking about the same woman who used to cower whenever our father walked into a room? That woman never asserted herself a day in her life."

Jane's brows drew together at the memory. "Father was a tyrant, but I've come to see another side of our mother since his passing. She was very happy when you returned home and didn't want to press the matter when you visited her in Suffolk, but

I fear her patience is at an end. She's set her mind on seeing you settled in the very near future."

"She can't force me to wed."

"She can try. She'll want you to be happily situated, of course, but be prepared to be subjected to a parade of England's most eligible young women over the next few months."

"Taking up residence elsewhere is looking more attractive." Or he could leave London altogether. He dismissed that idea almost as soon as it occurred to him. Cranston was in town, as was Lowenbrock and his new wife. He'd been looking forward to spending more time with the men who'd been his closest friends during the past few years of their fight against Napoleon. Certain he could manage his mother's attempts to marry him off, he wouldn't quit the battlefield so soon.

Jane lowered her voice and leaned forward in her chair. "You really don't want to leave Mother here all by herself."

Her words brought forth a pang of guilt that he did his best to ignore. "I know this is her first time staying in the house since Father passed, but I'm sure she'll be fine."

She arched a brow. "So you won't mind when she selects your future wife without any input from you and invites her to stay here? I'm sure she'll love telling everyone you've moved out of the town house to allow her time to get to know her future daughter-in-law."

He could only stare at his sister for several seconds, horror settling over him as he pictured that scenario playing out. After what felt like an eternity, he shook his head, but the image refused to leave his thoughts. "She wouldn't do that. And don't put the idea into her head."

"I wouldn't have to. Lady Herschel did that three years ago to force her reluctant son to wed."

He could actually feel the color drain from his face and found himself at a loss for words.

"So let me help you. I know a good number of suitable young women. We can have you betrothed by the end of the season without causing a scandal. Just tell me what type of woman you'd prefer."

He crossed his arms over his chest and scowled at his sister. "No, absolutely not. I have no intention of getting leg-shackled anytime soon."

"Which is precisely why I am here."

Ashford winced at the soft yet determined voice coming from the doorway and rose to his feet. After taking a moment to school his expression, he turned to face his mother.

The Dowager Viscountess Ashford swept into the room and engulfed him in a hug, the scent she'd favored since he was a boy wrapping around him. It threw him off-balance that his mother was now so effusive in showing affection. She'd always been reserved when he was younger, but that must have been for his father's benefit. Heaven knew the man had never liked him.

Despite the visible signs she was growing older, his mother was still a beautiful woman. When she pulled back, he couldn't help but notice the fine lines around her eyes and the lines that bracketed her mouth. Even her dark hair was becoming streaked with gray. But somehow those signs that she was no longer the flawless beauty he'd known growing up did nothing to diminish her appearance. She still looked beautiful in her lavender gown, a color he remembered her wearing often.

She clasped her hands at her waist and frowned up at him. "Now that's enough nonsense. You're almost thirty, and it's time for you to begin securing the family's future."

It took a great deal of effort to hold back his snort of amusement. "I was under the impression Father wanted Henry's children to inherit. That can still happen if I don't wed."

He'd long since come to terms with the fact that his father preferred his younger brother to him. If the previous Viscount Ashford could have declared Henry his heir, he would have done so long ago. His father had never come right out and said as much to him, but the man's constant criticism had made it clear.

That and the fact that his father hadn't cared when his heir declared his intention to enlist. His father had even gone out of his way to purchase him a commission the very next day.

His mother's lips pressed together in a firm line and she looked away, but not before he detected a hint of pain in her eyes. When she met his gaze again after several moments, it was as though she'd donned a mask.

"Your brother is not the Viscount Ashford. You are."

He lifted one shoulder in a shrug. "That doesn't mean he can't secure the line through his children."

"Henry won't be having children."

That was an odd statement. He opened his mouth to question her further, but Jane laid a hand on his arm to stop him. He met his sister's gaze, and she shook her head. There was definitely something here that neither his mother nor his sister wanted to talk about. Had his brother had an accident that rendered him incapable of performing sexually? He winced inwardly at the thought and let the subject drop.

His mother moved to his side and took his arm. "We can discuss this further over dinner," she said as she turned them toward the door. "I've been told you haven't even looked at the invitations you've received. Now that I'm here, I'll handle matters and ensure you're seen at only the most sought-after events. Your wife must be a woman of impeccable breeding. I'll start making inquiries in the morning as to which families are in town."

He cast a pleading glance at his sister, hoping she would say something to curtail his mother's determination.

Instead, Jane smiled at him and joined forces with their mother. "I've already started a list. We can compare notes."

©2022 Suzanna Medeiros

BOOKS BY SUZANNA MEDEIROS

Dear Stranger

Forbidden in February (A Year Without a Duke multi-author series)

Anthologies:

The Novellas: A Collection

Hathaway Heirs: Books 1-4

Landing a Lord: Books 1-3

Landing a Lord series:

Dancing with the Duke

Loving the Marquess

Beguiling the Earl

The Unaffected Earl

The Unsuitable Duke

The Unexpected Marquess

The Unwilling Viscount

The Baron's Return (Coming next!)

Christmas Scandals series:

A Viscount for Christmas

A Highwayman for Christmas

Hathaway Heirs series:

Lady Hathaway's Proposal

Lord Hathaway's Bride

Captain Hathaway's Dilemma

Miss Hathaway's Wish

For more information please visit the author's website:
https://www.suzannamedeiros.com/books/

ABOUT SUZANNA

USA Today bestselling author Suzanna Medeiros was born and raised in Toronto, Canada. Her love for the written word led her to pursue a degree in English Literature from the University of Toronto. She went on to earn a Bachelor of Education degree but graduated at a time when no teaching jobs were available. After working at a number of interesting places, including a federal inquiry, a youth probation office, and the Office of the Fire Marshal of Ontario, she decided to pursue her first love—writing.

Suzanna is married to her own hero and is the proud mother of twin daughters. She is an avowed romantic who enjoys spending her days writing love stories.

She would like to thank her parents for showing her that love at first sight and happily ever after really do exist.

To learn about Suzanna Medeiros's future books
(and to receive a bonus short story!) sign up for her
newsletter:
https://www.suzannamedeiros.com/newsletter

Visit her website:
https://www.suzannamedeiros.com

Or visit her on Facebook:
https://www.facebook.com/
AuthorSuzannaMedeiros

www.ingramcontent.com/pod-product-compliance
Lightning Source LLC
Chambersburg PA
CBHW022058050726
47591CB00002B/604